Snow White and the Seven Dwarfs

Book and Lyrics by
Elsa Rael

Music by
Michael Valenti

A Samuel French Acting Edition

SAMUELFRENCH.COM

IMPORTANT BILLING AND
CREDIT REQUIREMENTS

All producers of SNOW WHITE AND THE SEVEN DWARFS must give credit to the Authors in all programs distributed in connection with performances of SNOW WHITE AND THE SEVEN DWARFS, as well as in any and all advertising and publicity. The names of Elsa Rael and Michael Valenti must be in size of type not less than 50% of the size of type accorded the title. Billing for SNOW WHITE AND THE SEVEN DWARFS must be as follows:

(Name of Producer)
presents the musical play

"SNOW WHITE AND THE SEVEN DWARFS"

Book and Lyrics by   Music by
ELSA RAEL   MICHAEL VALENTI

The Gingerbread Players and Jacks' production of SNOW WHITE AND THE SEVEN DWARFS opened at New York's Theatre East on December 18, 1965 and ran for over three years. It had the longest continuous performance record of any children's show on or off Broadway. More than a million children have seen this work in live performance:

The Gingerbread Players and Jacks'
production of

SNOW WHITE AND THE SEVEN DWARFS

book and lyrics by
ELSA RAEL

music by
MICHAEL VALENTI

costumes by
Dick Leonard

sets by
Jack Logan

lighting by
Daniel Chodus

orchestration,
musical direction,
and musical numbers staged by
MICHAEL VALENTI

directed by
JOHN AHEARN

ORIGINAL NEW YORK CAST

Cast (In order of appearance)

THE QUEEN . . .... DANA ALEXIS ZELLER

SNOW WHITE .. . .SUSAN GEOPPINGER

THE MIRROR ... ...HIMSELF

THE WOODSMAN . .. . KEITH BAKER

SCRUBBER ... . KEVIN OWENS

BLUBBER . . . .GREGORY FRANK

SCOTTY ... ...ANDREI WOCJEK

FLUBBER ....STEVE BLOOM

PEPITO... . ... MARTIN RIVERA

MOSQUITO .. . . ALAN CORAO

FRED .. .. .BRET SMILEY

THE PRINCE . . .. KEITH BAKER

LOS ANGELES PRODUCTION
Opened April 2, 1985

Amanda Stone

in association with

Dishi Productions

presents

The Gingerbread Players and Jacks'

production of

Snow White and The Seven Dwarfs

music by
MICHAEL VALENTI

book and lyrics by
ELSA RAEL

Starring

KAYE BALLARD
as "The Queen"

CHRISTINE ANDREAS
as "Snow White"

with

ROD LOOMIS
as "The Woodsman"

AMICK BYRAM
as "The Prince

also co-starring (in alphabetical order)

Joseph Baham   Trevor Bullock   Dennis Courtney
Gregory Etheart   Michael Jay-Lawrence   Brian Ramage
David Anthony Silveira

costumes by
Dick Leonard

sets by
Jack Logan

lighting by
Lennie Del Luca Jr

*orchestration and
musical numbers by*
Michael Valenti

musical direction by
Steven Smith

choreography by
Jill Choder

directed by
JOHN AHEARN

LOS ANGELES PRODUCTION
Cast (In order of appearance)

The Queen	KAYE BALLARD
Snow White	CHRISTINE ANDREAS
The Mirror	HIMSELF
The Woodsman	ROD LOOMIS
Scrubber	JOSEPH BAHAM
Blubber	MICHAEL JAY-LAWRENCE
Scotty	DENNIS COURTNEY
Flubber	DAVID ANTHONY SILVEIRA
Pepito	GREGORY ETHEART
Mosquito	BRIAN RAMAGE
Fred	TREVOR BULLOCK
The Prince	AMICK BYRAM

for
Jody, Matthew, Gerard,
Rebecca, Benjamin and Galadriel

Time The Middle Ages
Place A Far Off Kingdom
Musical Numbers

Act I

Overture   Orchestra

Scene 1
(The Queen's Chamber)

Is The Maiden Tired?   The Queen and Snow White

Scene 2
(The Forest)

I'm Alive   Snow White and The Woodsman
A Lullaby   The Woodsman

Scene 2a
(The Cottage)

The Name Song   The Dwarfs and Snow White
I Never Had A Friend Before   Snow White and The Dwarfs
The Name Song (reprise)

Scene 3.
(The Queen s Chamber)

Look At Me   The Queen
Finale Act I   The Queen

15 Minute Intermission

Act II

Scene 4

(The Cottage)

Eat An Egg for Breakfast   Snow White and The Dwarfs
I'm Real Glad   Fred and Snow White
Pretty Things   The Old Woman
I Never Had A Friend Before (reprise)   Snow White and The Dwarfs

Scene 5
(The Queen s Chamber)

Scene 6
(The Cottage)

The Yodel Song   Snow White and The Dwarfs
The Dream Ballet   The Company

Scene 7
(The Forest)

A Promise Kept   The Prince
Finale   The Company

MUSIC CUES — COMPLETE LIST

No.		Page
1	PRELUDE	11
2	IS THE MAIDEN TIRED?	11
2a	The Brew	15
3	Change of scene	16
4	I'M ALIVE!	17
4a	Dance	18
4b	Reprise	18
5	A LULLABY	19
6	The Entrance of the Dwarfs	20
6a	Snow White Awakens	22
6b	The Tree House	22
7	THE NAME SONG	24
8	I NEVER HAD A FRIEND BEFORE	26
9	Finale Scene II (THE NAME SONG — reprise)	28
10	LOOK AT ME	28
11	The Sash	30
12	LOOK AT ME reprise	30
13	Change of scene	31
14	EAT AN EGG FOR BREAKFAST	31
14a	Going to work	33
15	I'M REAL GLAD	34
16	PRETTY THINGS	35
17	The Chase	36
18	Talk to us!	37
19	Saved!	37
20	I NEVER HAD A FRIEND BEFORE reprise	37
21	Change of scene	38
22	The Apple	39
22a	The Brew	39
23	Change of scene	40
24	THE YODEL SONG	41
24a	THE YODEL SONG encore	42
25	End of scene	45
26	DREAM BALLET	45
27	Doom	47
28	A PROMISE KEPT	48
29	FINALE	49
30	Finale Ultimo (curtain calls)	50
31	EXIT MUSIC	51

Snow White and the Seven Dwarfs

[MUSIC NO. 1: PRELUDE]

SCENE 1

The QUEEN's chamber.
The QUEEN is alone onstage, her back to the audience, hands
on hips to indicate impatience. She spins around and stares
accusingly into the audience.

QUEEN. Where are my slippers? That careless girl never lays
my things out properly. (*calling:*) Snow White? Snow White!
SNOW WHITE. (*entering from behind unit* R.) Yes, Your Maj-
esty?
QUEEN. What have you done with my slippers?
SNOW WHITE. You told me to brush them, Your Majesty.
QUEEN. And what took you so long?
SNOW WHITE. I was gone but a moment, Your Majesty.
QUEEN. Well let's not waste another. [MUSIC NO. 2: IS THE
MAIDEN TIRED?] Did you use the special polish I gave you?
SNOW WHITE. Yes, Your Majesty.
QUEEN. (*sits*) Help me on with them, dear.
SNOW WHITE. Yes, Your Majesty.

(*SNOW WHITE kneels to adjust the QUEEN's slippers. The*
QUEEN lifts SNOW WHITE's chin, and looks squarely into
her face, as she sings:)

QUEEN.
IS THE LITTLE MAIDEN WEARY?
SNOW WHITE.
NO, MY QUEEN, I'M HERE TO SERVE YOU
QUEEN.
HOW IS THAT?
SNOW WHITE.
TO CLEAN THE PALACE
QUEEN.
CLEAN IT WELL
FOR I'LL OBSERVE YOU.

11

IS THE LITTLE MAIDEN TIRED?
IS HER LIFE A BIT TOO BUSY?
   SNOW WHITE.
NO, YOUR HIGHNESS,
I'M WELL, TRULY
   QUEEN.
WON'T THIS LABOR MAKE YOU DIZZY?
YES, MY DEAR,
THIS I FEAR . . . (*She stands.*)
   SNOW WHITE. (*spoken:*) Please, Your Majesty, I'm perfectly well.
   QUEEN. (*spoken:*) In that case. . . . (*sings:*)
SET THE TABLE
SWEEP THE STABLE
SCRUB THE TURRET
AND THE GABLE
BOIL THE NOODLES
BRUSH THE POODLES
PARE THE APPLES
FOR THE STRUDELS
MIX THE BATTER
CHURN THE BUTTER
SHINE THE PLATTER
CLEAR THE CLUTTER
POLISH ALL THE SILVER SERVICE
STAND UP STRAIGHT
YOU MAKE ME NERVOUS!

SHAVE THE TINDERS
SWEEP THE CINDERS
PLUCK THE TURKEY
(*spoken:*) Work-ee, work-ee
HANG THE TOWELS
STUFF THE FOWLS
PLANE THE LUMBER
INTO DOWELS
SPICE THE CHILI
FEED THE FILLY
CUT THE CORN
FOR PIC-A-LILLY
STEW THE BERRIES

PIT THE CHERRIES
PEEL THE PEARS
RIGHT NOW!

(*SNOW WHITE begins to exit* L., *but the QUEEN stops her
    and continues:*)

I TRUST YOU NOTED
ALL I ASSIGNED YOU
I'LL NOT ABIDE
A PALACE UNCLEAN
UNLESS YOU PUT THESE
DUTIES BEHIND YOU
I CAN BECOME A
VERY MEAN QUEEN!
    SNOW WHITE. (*spoken:*) I know, Your Majesty.
    QUEEN. (*spoken:*) What?
    SNOW WHITE. I've noted all you assigned me, Your Majesty.
    QUEEN. Good. Now, then . . . (*sings:*)
FIX THE SHOWER
IN THE TOWER
STOKE THE FIRE
IN THE SPIRE
MEND THE CASEMENT
IN THE BASEMENT
DON'T FORGET TO
CUT THE BRIAR
WASH THE WINDOWS
SYSTEMATIC
FROM THE CELLAR
TO THE ATTIC
TILL MY BEAUTY
IS PROJECTED
IN A THOUSAND
PANES REFLECTED

THEN GO PLUCK
A PERFECT ROSE
TO TITILLATE
THE ROYAL NOSE
(*SNOW WHITE again begins to exit.*)
WAIT!

CHANGE THAT TO
A FULLSOME BUNCH
THEN YOU MAY
PREPARE MY LUNCH!
(*spoken:*) Then, I'll give you the afternoon work schedule.
   Snow White. Yes, Your Majesty.
   Queen. Now, prepare my mirror.
   Snow White. Oh, yes.
   Queen. Yes, *what?*
   Snow White. (*curtsies*) Yes, Your Majesty.

(*SNOW WHITE opens the shutters to reveal the MAGIC MIR-
ROR, curtsies again and exits* d.l.)

   Queen. What is it about that child I can't stand? (*walks to
mirror and preens*) My, don't I look marvelous today? Or am I
merely stunningly beautiful? I'm just too beautiful for words,
am I not? Tell me, Mirror, on the wall, who's the fairest of them
all?
   Mirror. (*MUSIC under.*)
     I answer Queen at your command
     Snow White's the fairest in the land . . .
(*Chord. MUSIC out.*)
   Queen. I trust you are aware this is the fourth time this week
you've lied to me?
   Mirror. (*MUSIC under.*)
     I never lie, my lovely Queen
     Snow White's the fairest to be seen . . .
(*Chord. MUSIC out*)
   Queen Ridiculous! Pure poppycock! Wait! Hold your judge-
ment, dear Mirror. This will change your mind, I'm sure. (*takes
perfume atomizer and sprays herself*) Mirror, Mirror on the
wall, who *now* is fairest of them all?
   Mirror. (*MUSIC under.*)
     Perfume and paint do not persuade
     Snow White is now the fairest maid   .
(*Chord. MUSIC out.*)
   Queen. Snow White, Snow White, Snow White! Is that all
you can say?
   Mirror. (*MUSIC under.*)
     A gentle grace, a smile so bright

A youthful charm all say Snow White . . .
(*Chord. MUSIC out.*)

QUEEN. You say she is more lovely than I? No, no, it cannot, must not be! I will not share my throne of beauty with another! Never! But what am I to do? I must do something. I must . . . I must . . . (*An idea is taking shape.*) Yes, I will be rid of her. Quite rid of her! But how? Help me, Mirror. Tell me, Mirror, what to do, to be the fairest in your view?

MIRROR. (*MUSIC under.*)
    You must prepare a sleeping foam
    To pour upon a magic comb
    Then send her to the forest deep
    And let her there forever sleep!
(*Chord. MUSIC out.*)

QUEEN. Marvelous. Simply marvelous. Oh, Mirror, you are as brilliant as I am beautiful. But wait, who will do the deed? And how will it be done?

MIRROR. (*MUSIC under.*)
    Send a woodsman with the maid
    Deep into a forest glade
    He'll place the comb and then he'll leave her
    Fast asleep with none to grieve her . . .
(*Chord. MUSIC out.*)

QUEEN. Wonderful! But how shall I make this sleeping foam?

[MUSIC NO. 2A: THE BREW]

MIRROR.
    Take the feather of a boa
    Mix it with green protozoa
    Add a dash of fertilizer
    Filtered through an atomizer
    Boil the scales of armadilla
    With a dash of sassparilla
    Dip the comb into this brew
    Snow White will sleep forever through!

(*As the MIRROR recites the recipe for the sleeping brew, the lights change to red, and the QUEEN mimes the preparation of the potion. On completion of the MIRROR's recitation, the QUEEN holds aloft the poisoned comb in triumph. She*

*claps her hands sharply three times, and the WOODSMAN
appears, as though by magic,* D R., *and bows. MUSIC out.*)

QUEEN. Here already, Woodsman? Good. I have a chore for
you. A task not altogether pleasant, but then . . .
WOODSMAN. Your wish is my command, Majesty. (*Bowing,
he is about to kiss her ring, but the QUEEN pulls away, with a
dismissive flip of her hand.*)
QUEEN Good. You are to take Snow White into the forest . .

(*QUEEN moves to* C. *Lights change to night, as her chamber
rolls off* L. *The WOODSMAN follows her, listening for his
orders. MUSIC under.*)

QUEEN. (*continued*) . . . deep, deep into the forest. And,
when you are certain no one is about, you are to run this comb
through her hair. (*She moves expressively to illustrate her statement.*)
WOODSMAN. And. . . ?
QUEEN. And? And? (*She runs off* U.L., *the sound of her evil
laughter echoing after her.*)

SCENE 2

[MUSIC NO. 3: CHANGE OF SCENE]

The Forest.
The scene is already underway as the QUEEN exits.
*The lights slowly change, revealing the exterior forest set. There
is fog, if possible. The shuttered cottage of the DWARFS is
built into the large central tree, but for the moment it is in-
distinguishable from the other trees, because of the closed
doors. The sound of chirping birds is heard. It is just before
dawn. The WOODSMAN is alone onstage, as if he had run
ahead of the following SNOW WHITE, seeking the place
where SNOW WHITE will meet her end.*

SNOW WHITE. Not so fast, Woodsman. We've walked for
hours and I'm tired.
WOODSMAN. Just a little further, Snow White. Just a few more
steps.

SNOW WHITE. Can't we rest? It's so pretty here, and I'm so very tired.

WOODSMAN. I think this is far enough into the forest. Yes, we'll rest here. This looks like a good place to . . . rest. (*The comb is now visible to the audience, and he tries to distract her.*) Listen, Snow White. Do you hear the pretty birds in the trees?

SNOW WHITE. Oh, hear them chatter and sing! Listen!

WOODSMAN. I believe they're singing a carol for you, Snow White! (*He attempts, but is still unable to use the comb on the unsuspecting SNOW WHITE, as she runs* D.R.

SNOW WHITE. And the breeze! Can you feel the sweet wind on your face, and the air is so fresh and clean! [MUSIC NO. 4: I'M ALIVE] (*She sings:*)

I'M ALIVE AND I'M BURSTING WITH SPRING!
I LOVE HEARING THE SONG
THAT THE LARKS LIKE TO SING
SEE THE DANDELIONS WINKING
THE BOBS BOB-O-LINKING
AND I'M FLYING HIGH WITHOUT WINGS!

(*She crosses* D.L.)

I'M ALIVE! I CAN JUMP! I CAN RUN!
I LOVE WATCHING THE DAISIES
THAT WAVE AT THE SUN
(*crosses* D.R. *to WOODSMAN*)
I LOVE DANCING ON DEW DROPS
AND CARTWHEELS AND FLIP-FLOPS
AND WHY DO I LIKE IT? IT'S FUN!

(*The WOODSMAN attempts to place comb, but SNOW WHITE turns to face him, foiling the attempt.*)

WAKE UP!
OPEN YOUR EYES
OR YOU'LL NEVER KNOW WHAT YOU'VE MISSED
WAKE UP!
HEY LOOK! SURPRISE!
THERE'S MORE TO THIS LIFE THAN
JUST MERELY EXIST . . . ING!

I'M ALIVE AND I'M HAPPY AND FREE!
I'M SO HAPPY INSIDE

THAT I'M SINGING FOR ME!
(*moving* DS.C.)
LOOK! THE MORNING IS BREAKING!
THE WHOLE WORLD IS WAKING!
THE SUN IS ABOUT TO ARRIVE!
I'M ALIVE! I'M ALIVE!
I'M ALIVE!

(*All during the song, the WOODSMAN has tried to find his chance to use the comb, but has been unable to catch SNOW WHITE still enough. At the end of the song, he's finally over her, menacing her with the comb. It should be a moment of horror, as he stands threateningly poised over her, then suddenly turns away.*)

WOODSMAN. I can't. I can't go through with it! Forgive me!
SNOW WHITE. Forgive you? But why? What have you done?
WOODSMAN. Forgive me for what I was about to do. The Queen ordered me to take you deep into the forest . . . and . . . I was to run the comb through your hair and then leave you. The magic of the comb would make you sleep forever. (*tosses comb* US. *to log*)
SNOW WHITE. But why? What have I done?
WOODSMAN. Your crime is being beautiful, more beautiful than the Queen. For that she would punish you. But I can't do it. Forgive me, Snow White, forgive me. I never meant to . . . (*He is on his knees, begging forgiveness.*)
SNOW WHITE. I forgive you, Woodsman. Of course I forgive you.
WOODSMAN. But I was about to . . .
SNOW WHITE. Don't cry, Woodsman. Please. See, I'm alive!

[MUSIC NO. 4A: DANCE]

(*SNOW WHITE dances to the music of "I'm Alive!". During the dance, she teaches the WOODSMAN to waltz, as he protests his ability to do so. At the end, she executes a "grapevine". The WOODSMAN attempts to follow, but stumbles clumsily over his own feet into SHOW WHITE's arms. She helps him to the log. He sits as she sings:*)

I'M ALIVE AND I'M HAPPY AND FREE!

I'M SO HAPPY INSIDE
THAT I'M SINGING FOR ME!
LOOK! THE MORNING IS BREAKING!
THE WHOLE WORLD IS WAKING!
THE SUN IS ABOUT TO ARRIVE!
I'M ALIVE!
   WOODSMAN.
YOU'RE ALIVE!
   BOTH.
WE'RE ALIVE!

(*The moment is a happy one. On the final chord of the music,
they link arms and plop down onto the log. There, SNOW
WHITE picks up the comb which the WOODSMAN has
discarded.*)

SNOW WHITE. Woodsman! What will you tell the Queen?
WOODSMAN. (*takes comb from her hand*) I'll tell her the evil
deed is done. But you must promise, Snow White, never to
return to the palace.
SNOW WHITE. I promise never to return. Here, take my ring.
Give it to the Queen. Tell her you took it from my hand as I
slept. And thank you, Woodsman, for sparing my life.
WOODSMAN. You look tired, Snow White. Why don't you rest
now. I'll stay and watch until you fall asleep.
SNOW WHITE. Yes, I will rest now.

(*SNOW WHITE lays down on the log. The WOODSMAN
walks about, making certain SNOW WHITE is safe.
Assured, he goes US. behind the log, kneels over SNOW
WHITE and sings.*)

   WOODSMAN.
SLEEP, SNOW WHITE
AND DREAM THE DAY
A PRINCE WILL COME
FROM FAR AWAY

REST YOUR HEAD
AND DRY YOUR TEARS
AND DREAM THE DAY
YOUR PRINCE APPEARS

(*He rises, crosses* D.R.)

HE WILL COME WEARING
A CAPE OF GOLD
AND BUCKLES OF SILVER
YOUR FUTURE IS TOLD

(*He comes* L. *of log, back to SNOW WHITE, at which point
she falls asleep.*)

SO SLEEP, SNOW WHITE
THE TIME IS LATE
A PRINCE WILL COME
JUST WAIT, JUST WAIT,
JUST WAIT . . .

(*The WOODSMAN backs out, and waves farewell to the sleeping girl on the final chord. He exits as the music fades. No
movement for 15 seconds. All that is heard is a bird chirping. Then, we hear a "far-off" musical theme echoing:*)

[MUSIC NO. 6: THE ENTRANCE OF THE DWARFS]

(*It is the SEVEN DWARFS approaching.*)

   DWARFS. (*singing, offstage*)
WE ALWAYS LIKE TO YODEL . . .
WE ALWAYS LIKE TO YODEL . . .

WE ALWAYS LIKE TO YODEL
WE ALWAYS LIKE TO YODEL
IT'S SUCH A MERRY SOUND
IT'S HARD TO BE UNHAPPY
WHEN A YODEL IS AROUND

HUM – HUM – HO
HUM – HUM – HO
HUM – HUM – HO

(*The SEVEN DWARFS enter, preferably from the back of the
audience.*)

WE ALWAYS LIKE TO YODEL
WE ALWAYS LIKE TO YODEL
WE DO IT ALL DAY LONG
'CAUSE WHEN YOU YODEL
YOU WILL FIND
THAT NOTHING CAN GO WRONG!

HUM – HUM – HO
HUM – HUM – HO
HUM – HUM – HO

(*The DWARFS march around in darkness; all we can see are their little lanterns. They are about to enter their "tree cottage", turning off the lanterns, when the lights come up. SCRUBBER is the first to see SNOW WHITE.*)

SCRUBBER. (*shouts*) What's *that*??? (*Chord*)
BLUBBER. Whatever it is, it's asleep! (*Chord.*)
SCOTTY. (*Scottish accent*) Hoot, man, I think, (*chord*), I think, (*chord*). Ah ha! It's a *gurrrl!*
FLUBBER. A gurrrl?
MOSQUITO. A gurrrl?
SCRUBBER. A gurrrl?
PEPITO. (*Hispanic accent*) Eet look vary scary to me-ee.
FLUBBER. But what's a *gurrrrl?*
BLUBBER. Oh, he means a girl.
FLUBBER. But what's a girl?
PEPITO. Oh, it's a lady thing. Deen't you aver see one before?
FLUBBER. (*He repeats everything.*) See one before? See one before? See one before? No, what is it?
PEPITO. You know, a lady thing.
FLUBBER. A lady thing, a lady thing, a lady thing? Oh, it's a lady thing.
DWARFS. Shhh!
FRED. (*sneezes*).
SCOTTY. Wait! What was that? (*MUSIC; SCOTTY approaches FRED who is hiding.*)
MOSQUITO. It's only Fred. (*MUSIC.*)
SCOTTY. What you doin' over there, hiding like that?
BLUBBER. Leave him alone. You know he's bashful.
FLUBBER. You know he's bashful, you know he's bashful, you know he's bashful.

Scrubber. All this talking is making me tired.
Blubber. And hungry. (*starts to sit on SNOW WHITE*)
Scotty. Be careful, you foolish creature. She might be dangerous . . . (*Chord.*)
Scrubber. Scotty's right. You can't trust everyone who comes along. You must be very careful.
Flubber. Very careful very careful, very careful.
Mosquito. But she doesn't look as though she would hurt anyone.
Blubber. Hey, maybe she can cook. (*MUSIC.*)
Flubber. You know something?
Mosquito. What?
Flubber. I still don't know what it is.
Dwarfs. It's a girl! (*Chord.*) A girl! (*Chord.*) A girl! (*Chord.*)

(*SNOW WHITE had been disturbed and begins to stir. The lights come up on SNOW WHITE. The DWARFS scatter in fright, and hide. SNOW WHITE rises, as from a dream.*)

[MUSIC NO. 6A: SNOW WHITE AWAKENS]

Snow White. A handsome prince . . . in a golden cape. Oh, such a lovely dream . . . (*She stumbles over one of the DWARFS.*) Oh! Who are you?
Scotty. Better not be askin' tew many questions, lass.
Scrubber. (*jumps out*) That's right! You're the stranger here, not us!
Snow White. That's true. I am a stranger here. Do you live here? (*They nod. She looks about confused.*) Where? I don't see a house or anything.
Blubber. (*jumps out*) You're not supposed to see it, unless we want you to. (*points to trees*) We live over there.
Snow White. Where? I still don't see anything.
Flubber. (*jumps out and dashes to the tree-door*) Here! We live here! Come inside and be warm!

[MUSIC NO. 6B: THE TREE HOUSE]

(*FLUBBER and MOSQUITO open the doors; lights up to show the inside of the cottage within the tree. All the DWARFS present their home as SNOW WHITE backs DS. in surprise. FRED dashes from his hiding place to the inside of the cot-*

*tage, whirling past SNOW WHITE, spinning her about in
his effort to escape. SNOW WHITE laughs in delight as she
enters the cottage.*)

SNOW WHITE. Oh, how wonderful! I never would have seen it!
How clever you are, and lucky to have such a pretty house. Do
you children live here all alone?

(*PEPITO and MOSQUITO come out of hiding peeved with
SNOW WHITE's statement.*)

MOSQUITO. We *do* live here alone, but we are *not* children!
SCOTTY. Most emphatically *not!*
PEPITO. We are not children!
SNOW WHITE. (*scolds*) Well, if you're not children, there is
certainly no excuse for keeping such a messy house! My
gracious, look at all the dirty socks lying all about, and the dirty
dishes . . . it's just terrible!
SCRUBBER. (*as he hastily picks up*) It's true, it's true! She's
right! (*to SNOW WHITE:*) I'm always telling them, but I can't
clean up all by myself, can I?
SNOW WHITE. Not by yourself, but there's no reason your little friends can't help you, by each picking up his own belong-
ings! (*They pick up their lanterns and place them in the tree
stump box* c.) And besides, if you're not children, what are you?
FLUBBER. (*Dopily, he jumps on log.*) We're dwarfs. We mine
for gold.
SCOTTY. What did yew want to be tellin' her thot furrr yew
fewlish creature?
FLUBBER. Why not? We are dwarfs, aren't we?
SCOTTY. Yes, we're dwarfs, but now she'll be after stealin' our
treasure!
MOSQUITO. Maybe that's what she came for!
PEPITO. She came for our treasure!
SCRUBBER. You can't have our treasure!
FLUBBER. No, no! You can't have our treasure.
ALL. *No, No, No, No, No. No!*

(*They crowd menacingly around SNOW WHITE, shouting.
BLUBBER jumps onto log, jumping up and down for their
attention.*)

BLUBBER. Wait a minute! Wait a minute! *Wait! A! Minute!* Of course she didn't come to steal our treasure! What's the matter with all of you!

SCRUBBER. Well, how do we know?

PEPITO. What deeed you come for?

SNOW WHITE. I came because the Queen didn't want me in the palace anymore. She doesn't like me very much and she wanted to be rid of me.

FLUBBER. She sounds very selfish.

BLUBBER. I don't think I like this Queen very much.

SCOTTY. Does that mean you have no home, Lass?

SNOW WHITE. Yes, that's right.

MOSQUITO. It must be sad to be without a home and all.

PEPITO. Very sad.

SCRUBBER. What's your name?

SNOW WHITE. Snow White. And your name? And your name? And yours?

[MUSIC NO. 7: THE NAME SONG]

(*The DWARFS line up for SNOW WHITE, all except FRED, who's still hiding. She can see his bottom sticking out. She smiles, but says nothing.*
Each of the DWARFS demonstrates his name-trait in a few dance steps in his turn:)

SCRUBBER.
MY NAME IS SCRUBBER
I'M A RUB-A-DUB-DUBBER
I'M HAPPY WHEN EVERYTHING'S CLEAN!
(*dusts SNOW WHITE with feather mop*)

BLUBBER.
MY NAME IS BLUBBER
I'M A REGULAR GRUBBER
I ADMIT THAT I'M NOT VERY LEAN (*pats his stomach*)

SCOTTY.
MY NAME IS SCOTTY
FROM OLD BRIGADOONEY
(*does a Scottish heel-toe step*)

FLUBBER.
AND MY NAME IS FLUBBER
'CAUSE I'M SLIGHTLY LOONEY
(*does "bell-step," and in the process trips and falls*)

MOSQUITO.
I'M CALLED MOSQUITO
I'M AN ITCHER AND A SCRATCHER
MY ALLERGIES ARE SUCH A BORE
(*He scratches himself.*)

PEPITO.
AND I AM PEPITO
FROM SANTA BENITO
MY PAPA IS A BIG MATADOR!
    ALL.
OLE!
(*PEPITO does a tango with SNOW WHITE.*)

SNOW WHITE.
BUT ONE OF YOU IS MISSING
I THINK THAT HE'S A CUTE ONE
A VERY SMALL FELLOW
A VERY MINUTE ONE
WHERE CAN HE BE HIDING NOW
I WISH THAT I COULD SEE HIM NOW
    DWARFS.
HE'S HIDING THERE UNDER THE BED
    SNOW WHITE.
COME OUT, PLEASE, IT'S JUST ME
OH PLEASE, WON'T YOU TRUST ME?
COME OUT PLEASE AND TELL US YOUR NAME?

(*FRED scampers out and announces while bashfully hiding
    his head.*)

FRED.
I'M FRED!

SNOW WHITE. (*spoken*) I'm glad to meet you, Fred.
DWARFS. He's bashful.

SNOW WHITE. Oh, I know just how he feels. I'm bashful, too, sometimes.

DWARFS. You? Bashful? (*They laugh among themselves.*)

SNOW WHITE. Oh, yes, it's really true. Whenever I'm with the Queen, I never know what to say. I just stand there feeling silly and shy. But I guess I won't have that problem anymore, now that I no longer live at the palace.

PEPITO. I don't think I like thees Queen very much.

SCOTTY. Well I definitely dinna like her.

SCRUBBER. Neither do I.

FLUBBER. Nor I.

BLUBBER. I don't like her, either.

MOSQUITO. No!

ALL. We like . . . you . . .

SNOW WHITE. It's very kind of you to say so . . . [MUSIC NO. 8: I NEVER HAD A FRIEND BEFORE] . . . and it's been so much fun being here with all of you. I'll never forget you. (*sings:*)

I NEVER HAD A FRIEND BEFORE
AND SO I NEVER KNEW
HOW VERY MUCH I NEEDED ONE
TILL I MET ALL OF YOU

THE MORE I LIVE, THE MORE I LEARN
HOW NICE A FRIEND CAN BE
THE MORE I LEARN THE MORE I KNOW
WHAT FRIENDSHIP MEANS TO ME

I'M REALLY VERY GRATEFUL
FOR EVERYTHING YOU'VE DONE
YOU WELCOMED ME WITH KINDNESS
YOU DON'T GET FROM EVERYONE

I NEVER HAD A FRIEND BEFORE
AND SO I NEVER KNEW
HOW VERY MUCH I NEEDED ONE
TILL I MET ALL OF YOU

PEPITO. (*spoken*) You never had a friend before?

SNOW WHITE. No.

FLUBBER. Never? That's terrible, terrible. I mean really terrible.

SCRUBBER. I'm so happy you have us.

SCOTTY. And we have you, lass.

FRED. You never had a friend before? Really?

SNOW WHITE. (*sings:*)

I NEVER HAD A FRIEND BEFORE

DWARFS.

AHH . . .

SNOW WHITE.

SO IF YOU NEED ME, TOO

DWARFS.

AHH . . .

SNOW WHITE.

JUST CALL MY NAME AND I WILL COME

YES, I WILL COME TO YOU . . .

DWARFS.

SNOW WHITE, SNOW WHITE . . .

SNOW WHITE.

YES, I WILL RUN TO YOU . . .

DWARFS.

NEVER HAD A FRIEND

NO, NEVER HAD A FRIEND . . .

SNOW WHITE.	DWARFS.
. . . TO YOU.	. . . BEFORE.

SNOW WHITE. Well, I guess it's time for me to go now . . . Goodbye . . . (*She starts to leave.*)

DWARFS. Snow White?

SNOW WHITE. Yes?

MOSQUITO. We thought maybe . . . ? maybe . . . ? you would . . . ? (*MOSQUITO begins to scratch an uncontrollable all-over itch, and is soon helped with the scratching by several of the others.*)

PEPITO. Maybe you would like to . . .

SCOTTY. Oh, hoot mon. We thought maybe yew would be willin' tew stay.

BLUBBER. And cook for us.

SCRUBBER. And help us with the cleaning.

PEPITO. And help us with the washing and scrubbing.

BLUBBER. And cook for us.

FLUBBER. And help us make the beds, make the beds, make . . .

BLUBBER. And cook for us.

SCRUBBER. And keep the fire going.

MOSQUITO. And scratch my back.

BLUBBER. And cook for us.

SCOTTY. And sing to us.

PEPITO. And read to us.

BLUBBER. And cook for us. And cook for us. And cook . . . for . . . us. (*The other DWARFS laugh.*)

DWARFS. Won't you stay? Please won't you stay?

[MUSIC NO. 9: THE NAME SONG (REPRISE)]

SNOW WHITE. (*sings:*)
YOU'RE ASKING ME TO STAY HERE
TO WORK WITH YOU AND PLAY HERE
YOU'RE A LITTLE MESSY
BUT I WILL SAY IT'S GAY HERE
DWARFS.
AND WE WILL BEFRIEND YOU
PROTECT AND DEFEND YOU
FRED.
AND EVERYDAY WILL BE A HOLIDAY!
SNOW WHITE.
I'D COOK AND I'D DUST UP
AND CLEAN WHAT IS MESSED UP
DWARFS.
OH, PLEASE TELL US WHAT DO YOU SAY?
(*paces while she decides*)
SNOW WHITE.
I'LL STAY!
DWARFS.
YAY!

(*Blackout*)

SCENE 3

The QUEEN's chamber.
The QUEEN is seated on her throne, looking very pleased with
*   herself.*

[MUSIC NO. 10: LOOK AT ME]

QUEEN.
LOOK AT ME
I'M SO FAIR
MY BEAUTY EVEN FADES
THE MORNING GLARE

AND I'M SO LOVELY
AND BEYOND COMPARE
I CAN'T HELP SINGING TO MYSELF!

LOOK AT ME
I BEGUILE
AND HAVE YOU EVER SEEN
A SWEETER SMILE?
OH, I'M SO ELEGANT
AND I HAVE STYLE
I CAN'T HELP SINGING TO MYSELF!

MY BEAUTY WALKS IN GRACE AND SPLENDOR
MY BEAUTY RULES THE DAY
WHEN SNOW WHITE DARED TO THREATEN ME
I HAD HER PUT . . . A . . . WAY . . .

NOW, LOOK AT ME
I'M STILL QUEEN
I'M STILL THE LOVELIEST
MY EYES HAVE EVER SEEN
OH, TELL ME,
MIRROR, MIRROR ON THE WALL
WHO NOW IS FAIREST OF THEM ALL?
Pray tell
WHO NOW IS FAIREST OF THEM ALL?
Oh, well!
WHO NOW IS FAIREST OF THEM ALL?!

MIRROR.
     I answer, Queen, at your command:
     Snow White's the fairest of the land.
QUEEN. Oh, no, dear Mirror. I think you are reflecting the wrong information this time. Take another look. Or are you merely teasing me with an itsey-bitsey little white lie?
MIRROR.
     I cannot tell a lie, my Queen.
     Snow White's the fairest to be seen.
QUEEN. Enough tomfoolery! I have here Snow White's ring which proves she is asleep in the forest forever.
MIRROR.
     The ring is but a mere contrive.

Snow White is well and quite alive.

QUEEN. Alive? Well, this teaches me a lesson. If I want something done, I must do it myself. Where is Snow White to be found?

MIRROR.
    She lives with seven little men
    In a lonely forest glen.

QUEEN. Oh, dreadful truth, vile truth, unhappy truth, why do you plague me?

MIRROR.
    I'm bound to tell the truth at once
    Regardless whom the truth affronts
    Truth is fact and fact is true
    Snow White is lovelier than you!

QUEEN. Then something must be done—and now. Tell me what to do, dear Mirror. Give me a plan that must not this time fail.

[MUSIC NO. 11: THE SASH]

MIRROR.
    A sash with magic thread you'll baste
    To put about the maiden's waist
    And when you have her tightly bound
    She'll never make another sound!

(*As the MIRROR gives his instruction, the QUEEN mimes the stitching of the sash. LIGHTS change to red.*)

QUEEN. Yes. Ah yes, a sash with magic thread. How marvelously sinister. (*Chord.*) How deliciously diabolical. (*Chord.*) How devilishly clever! (*Chord.*) How—mean! (*She sings:*)

[MUSIC NO. 12: LOOK AT ME (REPRISE)]

YES, BEAUTY WALKS IN GRACE AND SLENDOR
AND BEAUTY RULES THE DAY
WHEN SNOW WHITE DARES TO THREATEN ME
I'LL HAVE HER PUT A-WAY

LOOK AT ME

I'M STILL QUEEN
I'M STILL THE LOVELIEST
MY EYES HAVE EVER SEEN
OH MIRROR,
LOVELY MIRROR ON THE WALL
I'LL BE THE FAIREST OF THEM ALL!

(*Fast fadeout on the QUEEN's cackling laughter.*)

(If desired, an intermission may be placed at this point.)

[MUSIC NO. 13: CHANGE OF SCENE]

SCENE 4

The DWARF's Cottage. The next day.
SNOW WHITE and the DWARFS have just had breakfast.
SNOW WHITE is holding a frying-pan into which "egg
props" have been glued. The log now serves as a table, with
the DWARFS seated on the floor around it.

[MUSIC NO. 14: EAT AN EGG FOR BREAKFAST]

SNOW WHITE. (*sings:*)
EAT AN EGG FOR BREAKFAST
AND YOU CAN'T GO WRONG
SCRAMBLED, FRIED OR SUNNYSIDE
TO MAKE YOU GROW UP STRONG

EAT AN EGG FOR BREAKFAST
WITH MILK AND WHOLE WHEAT BREAD
PLAIN OR TOAST WHICH YOU LIKE MOST
TO KNOW THAT YOU'RE WELL-FED

(*She crosses* D.R.)

START YOUR DAY WITH NOURISHMENT
AND TAKE YOUR VITAMINS
YOUR DAY CAN ONLY BE FOR YOU
AS GOOD AS IT BEGINS

SEE THAT YOU GET LOTS OF REST
TO BUILD YOUR TEETH AND BONES
AND WITH THE PROPER EXERCISE
YOU'LL HEAR YOUR MUSCLE TONES
SO . . .

Dwarfs.
EAT AN EGG FOR BREAKFAST
EAT IT ANY WAY
Snow White.
POACHED OR MINCED OR GENTLY BLINTZED
BUT EAT AN EGG TODAY

All.
EAT AN EGG FOR BREAKFAST
TO START YOU WITH A GRIN
Snow White.
FEATHERED, FLICKED OR BENEDICT
YOUR DAY WILL THEN BEGIN

Dwarfs. (*standing*)
START YOUR MORNING WITH THE SMILE
OF EXTRA ENERGY
Fred. (*jumping on the log*)
WITH BACON, HAM OR CHERRY JAM
Two Dwarfs. (*on either side of FRED, on the log*)
JUST TRY OUR RECIPE
Snow White.
YOUR FRIENDS WILL WONDER AT YOUR STRENGTH
AND ASK YOU HOW IT'S DONE
YOU'LL SAY THE SECRET'S IN THE EGG
All.
YOU ONLY NEED BUT ONE . . .
Snow White. (*pretending to be an opera star*)
. . . AHHH . . .

(*As she completes her "cadenza," the DWARFS applaud.
SNOW WHITE calls them back to attention by clapping
sharply three times. The DWARFS form a straight line
across the stage in order of size, and all begin to march in
place, as they sing the following coda. On each line, SNOW
WHITE comes behind and taps the DWARFS one-by-one
on the head. As each DWARF is tapped, he steps forward*)

ALL.
EAT AN EGG FOR BREAKFAST
EAT IT ANY WAY
SCRAMBLED, FRIED OR SUNNYSIDE
POACHED, OR MINCED, OR GENTLY BLINTZED
FEATHERED, FLICKED OR BENEDICT
WITH BACON, HAM OR CHERRY JAM
HARD OR SOFT OR IN THE MIDDLE
IN THE PAN OR ON THE GRIDDLE
KEEPS YOU FITTER THAN A FIDDLE
  SNOW WHITE
EAT IT ANY WAY
  ALL.
BUT EAT AN EGG TODAY!
(*The DWARFS do a form of "patty-cake" clapping hands and thighs on tag line:*)
AN EGG TODAY!
(*All laugh happily and plop down, exhausted and full*)

SNOW WHITE. Anyone for seconds?
SCRUBBER. No, thank you.
FLUBBER. I'm full. I'm full. I'm full.
PEPITO. I've had enough, too.
SNOW WHITE. Scotty?
SCOTTY No, thank you, Lass. I've no room for more. But yew won't be throwin' away those leftover eggs, will yew now?
SNOW WHITE. Oh, no. I'll put them in a special pudding.
BLUBBER. Chocolate?
SNOW WHITE. Chocolate.
MOSQUITO. No. Not chocolate, please. It makes me itch! (*The very thought makes MOSQUITO itch and several of the DWARFS help him to scratch places he can't reach*)
SNOW WHITE. Oh, that's too bad. I know. I'll make a special little angel food cake just for you, Mosquito.
MOSQUITO. (*stops scratching*) For me? Oh, thank you.
SCOTTY. Enough of this talk. We'd best be gettin' to work.

[MUSIC NO. 14A: GOING TO WORK]

(*The DWARFS line-up for their goodbye kisses from SNOW WHITE. The order isn't important, just so FRED is last and SCOTTY next to last. SNOW WHITE kisses each on the forehead and they file off* R. *SCOTTY refuses a kiss, and of-*

*fers to shake hands instead. SNOW WHITE respects SCOT-
TY's preference, and they shake hands. FRED is about to
receive his kiss, but he runs shyly back to the log and sits.
SNOW WHITE realizes he wants to tell her something.)*

[MUSIC NO. 15: I'M REAL GLAD]

(*She walks to him, as he sings:*)

FRED.
I'M REAL GLAD WE FOUND YOU
I'M REAL GLAD YOU'LL STAY
I'M REAL GLAD AROUND YOU
PLEASE DON'T EVER GO AWAY

ARE YOU GLAD YOU LIVE HERE?
SNOW WHITE.
I'M REAL GLAD I DO
FRED.
THEN STAY WITH US FOREVER
SNOW WHITE.
I'M REAL GLAD TO BE HERE WITH YOU

SNOW WHITE AND FRED.
I'M GLAD YOU'RE REAL GLAD, TOO!

(*After a moment, FRED remembers the other DWARFS have
left, and calls after them:*)

FRED. Hey! Wait for me!

(*He is about to run-off, when he realizes he hasn't been kissed
by SNOW WHITE. FRED returns for the kiss, and runs
off.*)

SNOW WHITE. Aren't they just wonderful? Well, I guess it's
time to start cleaning up. (*sings a capella:*)
EAT AN EGG FOR BREAKFAST
AND YOU CAN'T GO WRONG
SCRAMBLED, FRIED OR SUNNYSIDE
TO MAKE YOU GROW UP . . .

(*SNOW WHITE is sweeping the floor when the QUEEN enters, disguised as the FIRST OLD WOMAN.*)

SNOW WHITE. Oh! I didn't know anyone was there!

[MUSIC NO. 16: PRETTY THINGS]

QUEEN. (*sings*)
IS THE LITTLE LADY STARTLED?
SNOW WHITE. (*sings*)
THAT'S ALL RIGHT. HOW MAY I AID YOU?
QUEEN.
LET ME SIT. MY BONES ARE WEARY (*sits*)
PLEASE FORGIVE IF I DISMAYED YOU.

IS THE LITTLE LADY FRIGHTENED?
SNOW WHITE.
I'LL NOT SPEAK UNLESS I KNOW YOU
QUEEN.
I'M A POOR AND TIRED GRANNY
SELLING TRINKETS
LET ME SHOW YOU:

I BAKE MUFFINS,
I SEW FRILLIES
CAPTURE PUFFENS
AND GROW LILLIES
I STITCH SMOCKING,
FIX OLD FLOCKING
BASTE A SEAM
AND DARN A STOCKING

I MEND POCKETS,
SING TO CRICKETS
OPEN LOCKETS,
SAVE OLD TICKETS
I MAKE NIFTY
LITTLE GIFTIES
AND FOR YOU—A SASH!
(*The QUEEN unfurls the long red sash, and offers it to SNOW WHITE.*) Isn't it pretty? And only tuppence. Would you like to try it on?

SNOW WHITE. Oh, it is pretty. I'd be happy to try it on.

QUEEN. (*adjusting sash on SNOW WHITE:*) It fits you to perfection. I might even say it was made to order for you. (*Drum roll.*)

(*The QUEEN pulls the sash and knots it tightly, as SNOW WHITE cries:*)

SNOW WHITE. Oh, it's too tight! It's taking my breath away! Loosen it quickly! I can't breathe! Help . . . me . . . please . . . help . .

(*SNOW WHITE faints and the QUEEN guides her to the log. The QUEEN laughs a laugh of evil triumph, when suddenly she hears the returning DWARFS.*
FRED enters D.R. *They freeze a moment and stare at each other. FRED turns and runs off* R.
The QUEEN laughs, returns to check SNOW WHITE, then exits D.L.
Suddenly, she re-enters, walking backwards slowly, as a few DWARFS advance, facing her. The QUEEN spins about, attempting to escape D.R., *but the other DWARFS are already advancing from that direction. She is backed to* C. *and confused, tries to exit* US. *of log, but is stopped by the stage* R. *DWARFS. She turns to go* L., *but is stopped by the stage* L. *DWARFS. She then bends down and sneaks past the stage* R. *DWARFS, who now run with the stage* L. *DWARFS. The QUEEN crosses and exits down* S.L. *and the CHASE begins—*)

[MUSIC NO. 17: THE CHASE]

(*Strobe on. In stylized slow motion, the DWARFS chase the QUEEN. At one point, the chase reverses and the QUEEN appears to chase the DWARFS. Suddenly, FRED stands* R. *of* C., *calling to the other DWARFS, ending the strobe.*)

FRED. Wait! Stop! We forgot about Snow White! She needs help!

(*The DWARFS halt the chase and gather around SNOW WHITE.*)

[MUSIC NO. 18: TALK TO US]

BLUBBER. What is it, Snow White?

MOSQUITO. She can't tell us. She can't talk.

FLUBBER. It must have been that wicked Queen, wicked Queen, wicked Queen.

SCOTTY. She must have done something terrible to Snow White.

PEPITO. What can we do?

SCRUBBER. She looks so pale.

FRED. I've been looking over the situation . . .

SCOTTY. And what do you think, Fred?

FRED. Well, the only thing different is the sash. She didn't have it on this morning when we left. Perhaps it's too tight.

FLUBBER. Too tight, too tight.

FRED. I think we should take it off.

SCOTTY. Do you really think so, Fred?

FRED. I do.

SCOTTY. All right, men. Remove the sash.

[MUSIC NO. 19: SAVED!]

(*TWO DWARFS remove the tucked end of the sash, and SNOW WHITE spins to unwind herself free of it.*)

SNOW WHITE. That sash was so tight . . . I couldn't breathe. You saved my life.

FLUBBER. Fred thought of it.

SNOW WHITE. Thank you, Fred.

FRED. But that's what friends are for. Isn't it? To help?

SNOW WHITE. Yes, Fred. And all of you, thank you. You're the kindest, sweetest people I've ever known. (*SNOW WHITE moves C. and sits. The DWARFS cluster around her on the floor and two on either side of her.*)

[MUSIC NO. 20: I NEVER HAD A FRIEND BEFORE (REPRISE)]

I'M REALLY VERY GRATEFUL
FOR EVERYTHING YOU'VE DONE
YOU WELCOMED ME WITH KINDNESS
YOU DON'T GET FROM EVERYONE

I NEVER HAD A FRIEND BEFORE
> DWARFS.
AHH . . .
SO IF YOU NEED ME, TOO
> DWARFS.
AHH . . .
> SNOW WHITE.
JUST CALL MY NAME AND I WILL COME
YES, I WILL COME TO YOU
> DWARFS.
SNOW WHITE, SNOW WHITE
> SNOW WHITE.
YES, I WILL RUN TO YOU . . .
> DWARFS.
NEVER HAD A FRIEND
NO, NEVER HAD A FRIEND . . .

SNOW WHITE.	DWARFS.
. . . TO YOU.	. . . BEFORE.

(*As the closing bars of the music fade, they all fall asleep, huddled about SNOW WHITE.*)

(*Slow fadeout*)

[MUSIC NO. 21: CHANGE OF SCENE]

SCENE 5

The QUEEN's chamber.
The QUEEN has just returned from her chase with the DWARFS, and she's still panting from running.

QUEEN. Did you see? Did you see the way they chased me? Ugly little gnarled creatures! Have they no respect for size? But I escaped them, and I accomplished the skullduggerous deed! That's all that matters. (*She cackles dementedly.*) They're probably weeping cute, adorable little dwarf tears over Snow White. Go see, dear Mirror. See and tell me what's happening right now, every deliciously diabolical detail.
MIRROR.
The plot misfired, and withal
Snow White's the fairest of them all.

QUEEN. (*screaming*) No, no, no, no, no! The plot was foolproof. You said so yourself. What could have happened? How did she escape the fate of that sash?

MIRROR.
    The sash was found, the knot undone
    Snow White is still the fairest one.

QUEEN. (*deflated*) Nothing, nothing, nothing to which I apply my genius for evil works in my behalf. Why?? Am I forever consigned to reign *second* in beauty? (*Enraged:*) No! I refuse to be thus dismissed! Something will be done, I promise! Some act of evil! (*Entreating:*) Please, dear Mirror, I beg a favor . . . a plan so wrought, so well-designed, so delicately manipulated as to demolish Snow White at once and forever!!

MIRROR.
    Give me but a moment, Queen
    To plan a plot to vent your spleen

QUEEN. Take your fiendish moment, but make it certain . . . (*Small pause. Three drum beats.*) Well?

MIRROR.
    Give me but a moment more
    I plan a strategy of gore

[MUSIC NO. 22: THE APPLE]

(*The MIRROR begins to laugh and the QUEEN soon joins in. The laughter builds until it verges on the hysterical; at its peak, the QUEEN stops abruptly to ask:*)

QUEEN. Yes, yes? Tell me!
MIRROR.
(*over MUSIC:*)
    You'll stir a poison sleeping brew
    And steep an apple there, into
    You'll give the fruit and she will bite
    Then ever will she know the dark of night!
QUEEN. And what are the ingredients of the poison brew?

[MUSIC NO. 22A: THE BREW TOO]

MIRROR.
    Take the molar of a spider
    Mix with brine of apple cider
    Prick the pinky of a panda

> Pickled gland of salamander
> Sauté tadpoles with an oxtail
> Stir it with a furry foxtail
> Dip the fruit in this bouquet
> Snow White won't see another day!

(*As the MIRROR lists the poison ingredients, the lights turn to red, and the QUEEN mimes the motions of mixing the brew. At the completion of the last line of the recipe, the QUEEN holds the poisoned apple aloft and avows, as the lights fade:*)

QUEEN. Snow White won't see another day!

[NO. 23: CHANGE OF SCENE]

SCENE 6

The DWARFS' cottage.
The DWARFS are lecturing SNOW WHITE before they leave for work. SNOW WHITE is seated on the log.

SCRUBBER. Now remember. You're not to let anyone in.
BLUBBER. You're too trusting. That's your problem.
SCOTTY. Yew have got to be more careful, Lass.
FLUBBER. Even *I* know you can't let everyone in who comes knocking at your door, knocking at your door, knocking at your door.
SNOW WHITE. You're absolutely right, Scrubber, Blubber, Scotty and Flubber. I'll be more careful, I promise.
PEPITO. And you won't talk to strangers?
SNOW WHITE. No, Pepito.
MOSQUITO. And you'll ask "who is it?" before you open the door?
SNOW WHITE. Yes, Mosquito.
FRED. And you won't open it unless it's someone you know?
SNOW WHITE. No, Fred, I promise. Oh, please, please don't look so unhappy. I can't let you go off to work looking so miserable and worried.
FLUBBER. We can't help it, Snow White. Can't help it, can't help it.
BLUBBER. We *look* miserable and worried . . .

SCRUBBER. Because we *are* miserable and worried.

SNOW WHITE. Isn't there anything I can do to make you happy? [MUSIC NO. 24: THE YODEL SONG] (*SNOW WHITE gets an idea, and sings:*)

YO-DEL-AI-DI-O
(*The DWARFS moan in response.*) What's the matter? (*She tries again. Sings:*)
YO-DEL-AI-DI-O
(*The DWARFS are weakening, giving in.*) Come on! (*SNOW WHITE tries again. Sings:*)
YO-DEL-AI-DI-O!

    DWARFS. (*laughing and joining the merriment*)
YO-DEL-AI-DI-O!

SNOW WHITE.
WE ALWAYS LIKE TO YODEL
WE ALWAYS LIKE TO YODEL
IT'S SUCH A MERRY SOUND
IT'S HARD TO BE UNHAPPY
WHEN A YODEL IS AROUND!

DWARFS.
YO-DEL-AI-DI-O
YO-DEL-AI-DI-O
YO-DEL-AI-DI
YO-DEL-AI-DI . . .
YO-DEL-AI-DI-O

SNOW WHITE.
WE ALWAYS LIKE TO YODEL
WE ALWAYS LIKE TO YODEL
WE DO IT ALL DAY LONG
'CAUSE WHEN YOU YODEL
YOU WILL FIND
THAT NOTHING CAN GO WRONG

DWARFS.
YO-DEL-AI-DI-O
YO-DEL-AI-DI-O
YO-DEL-AI-DI
YO-DEL-AI-DI . . .
YO-DEL-AI-DI-O

Snow White.
TRY A YODEL, TRY IT SLOW
    Dwarfs.
YO-DEL YO-DEL O-DEL O-DEL
YO-DEL-AI-DI-O
    Snow White
NOW GO FASTER — LET IT GO
    Dwarfs.
YO-DEL O-DEL YO-DEL O-DEL
YO-DEL O-DEL YO-DEL O-DEL
    All.
YO, AND AWAY WE GO!

Dwarfs	Snow White.
AND NOW THAT YOU CAN YODEL	AH . . . YODEL,
AND NOW THAT YOU CAN YODEL	AH . . . YODEL,

    All.
YOU'LL DO MOST ANYTHING
YOU'LL YODEL THROUGH YOUR WINTER
AND YOU'LL YODEL INTO SPRING!

(*If desired, a DANCE SECTION may be added at this point
    by repeating the accompaniment from the beginning of the
    chorus. Otherwise, continue as written:*)

    Dwarfs.
YO-DEL-AI-DI-O
YO-DEL-AI-DI-O
YO-DEL-AI-DI
YO-DEL-AI-DI . . .
YO-DEL-AI-DI-O!
    Snow White.
YO-DEL-AI-DI-O
YO-DEL-AI-DI-O
YO-DEL-AI-DI
YO-DEL-AI-DI . . .
    All.
YO-DEL-AI-DI-O-O-O-O
YO-DEL-AI-DI-O!

[MUSIC NO. 24A: THE YODEL SONG (ENCORE)]

(*The DWARFS march off in single file, continuing to yodel as they exit, as SNOW WHITE waves goodbye.*)

    DWARFS.
YO-DEL-AI-DI-O
YO-DEL-AI-DI-O
YO-DEL-AI-DI
YO-DEL-AI-DI . . .
    ALL.
YO-DEL-AI-DI-O-O-O-O
YO-DEL-AI-DI-O!
    SNOW WHITE.
BYE!

(*When the DWARFS are offstage, SNOW WHITE picks up the broom and begins to sweep as she, too, yodels a capella:*)

    SNOW WHITE. (*to herself*)
YO-DEL-AI-DI-O . . .
    QUEEN'S VOICE. (*offstage and sweetly*)
YO-DEL-AI-DI-O . . .

(*At the sound of the offstage voice, SNOW WHITE appears bewildered, goes indoors, but continues to yodel a capella.*)

    SNOW WHITE.
YO-DEL-AI-DI, YO-DEL-AI-DI . . .

(*The QUEEN, dressed as a SECOND OLD WOMAN enters, and with a raspy, awful voice this time, completes the yodel call:*)

    QUEEN/OLD WOMAN.
YO-DEL-AI-DI-O!

(*SNOW WHITE, frightened, hides behind the door of the house.*)

    OLD WOMAN. (*spoken:*) Hello?
    SNOW WHITE. Hello??
    OLD WOMAN. Hello???
    SNOW WHITE. Who are you?

OLD WOMAN. Just a poor old granny, out earning her daily bread. May I come in?

SNOW WHITE. I don't know. (*beat*) Do I know you?

OLD WOMAN. I don't think we've met before, but I can't tell for sure until I see you. Isn't that right?

SNOW WHITE. (*to herself:*) It sounds right, all right. (*to OLD WOMAN:*) Do you mean me any harm?

OLD WOMAN. Of course not. I don't even know you . . . . I think.

SNOW WHITE. (*to herself:*) That's right. If she doesn't know me, she can't mean me any harm, can she? (*to OLD WOMAN:*) You may come in.

OLD WOMAN. (*entering the house*) Hello, dearie. Oh my, what a nice little house you have here. And so clean.

SNOW WHITE. Thank you. I try to keep it that way.

OLD WOMAN. Are your seven little friends about?

SNOW WHITE (*suspicious*) I thought you said you didn't know me?

OLD WOMAN. But I don't.

SNOW WHITE. Then how did you know I have seven little friends?

OLD WOMAN. (*thinking fast, answering harshly:*) I saw seven little beds and figured it out.

SNOW WHITE. Oh. That was clever. To answer your question, no, my seven little friends are not about. They're out working. Can *I* do anything for you?

OLD WOMAN. Oh, no. I was just lonely and I thought wouldn't it be nice to share my lunch with somebody. (*In tears:*) Would you like to share my lunch?

SNOW WHITE. Do you have enough?

OLD WOMAN. More, more than enough for the both of us. See? I have two apples in my basket. One for me and one for . . . you. Here. Take it.

(*Drums. SNOW WHITE takes the apple and slowly raises it to her mouth. The MUSIC swells. SNOW WHITE quickly lowers her hand. MUSIC out.*)

OLD WOMAN. Eat it, dearie. It won't bite you.

(*Drums. Once more SNOW WHITE raises the apple to her mouth, then is unable to bite into it, and offers to return it to the OLD WOMAN.*)

SNOW WHITE. I'm really not hungry, thank you.
OLD WOMAN. *Bite it! Bite it, I say!*

(*SNOW WHITE bites the apple, and falls into a swoon. The OLD WOMAN guides the fainting girl to the log. SNOW WHITE lies there in the "sleep of forever." The triumphant QUEEN looks upward, as though addressing her MIRROR.*)

OLD WOMAN. Oh, Mirror, I would you were here beside me now to see this victory. We earned it together, you and I. No more will I hear the accursed words extolling another's beauty over mine. (*Chord.*) No more and nevermore! (*Chord.*) Once again I reign alone in beauty! (*MUSIC.*) Sleep a sleep of forever, Snow White, and dream your dreams that will never come true!

(*The QUEEN exits* U.L., *laughing maniacally.*)

[MUSIC NO. 25: END OF SCENE]

(*The lights fade to blue. It is night, and the BALLET begins in fog.*)

[MUSIC NO. 26: DREAM BALLET]

BALLET. The dance is inevitably sad, quickly recapping the story to this point in both dance and music.

SNOW WHITE begins to dream and slowly awakens. Her hand rises, as though someone has taken her by the hand and is leading her.
The PRINCE enters U.R., *bows to her; she bows to him,* D.L., *facing audience. Neither, however, looks at nor sees the other. (It should be clear to the audience SNOW WHITE has conjured the PRINCE in her dream.) They execute the same dance steps, but never touch.*
The PRINCE exits U.R.; *as SNOW WHITE becomes aware of his leaving, she reaches out toward the audience in supplication.*
The DWARFS enter, and dance a stylized version of the previous dance steps in dreamlike playfulness. SNOW WHITE

dances with them, but alone. They wave goodbye and exit
D R., as SNOW WHITE blows the DWARFS a goodbye kiss.
The QUEEN enters D.L. with an apple, this time grotesquely
huge as might occur in a nightmare. SNOW WHITE bites
the apple and falls into her original position on the log, as at
the beginning of the dance. The QUEEN exits silently.

INTO REALITY: Slowly, sadly, to the chiming of bells, the
DWARFS reenter from U.R. They bear flowered poles and
wreaths and a satin pillow. A pole is placed into each corner
of the log/bier. One of them lifts SNOW WHITE's head as
FRED places the pillow beneath it. Another straightens her
skirt, and a bouquet-wreath is placed in her clasped hands.
The LULLABY MUSIC plays under this scene and the ensuing
dialogue. As the DWARFS now speak, it is no longer a
dream but tragic reality.

BLUBBER. We never should have left her alone.
FRED. I knew something would happen. I knew it.
SCOTTY. Snow White-lass tell us what's the matter?
MOSQUITO. Where does it hurt, Snow White?
PEPITO. Tell us. Talk to us.
SCRUBBER. We never should have left her alone.
FLUBBER. We should have stayed right here with her.
FRED. Please come back to us, Snow White. We need you.
SCRUBBER. (*softer*) We need you . . .
BLUBBER. (*almost too soft to hear*) We need you . . .

(*The lights begin to fade.*)

DWARFS.
HUM HUM HO
HUM HUM HO
HUM . . . HUM . . . HO . . .

(*The lights dim to blue again. The stage is split into two areas,*
as a "special" comes up on the QUEEN talking to her MIR-
ROR:)

QUEEN. How dare you tell me because of my selfishness I'm no
longer beautiful! Ridiculous! I should have known better than to

confide in a stupid mirror! I *am* beautiful! (*Like a child:*) *I am beautiful!*

MIRROR.
> Once you walked in beauty, Queen
> But you changed all that by being mean
> Selfishness has spoiled your beauty
> It even kept you from your duty
> Conceit is yours, with hate to spare
> Now nevermore will you be fair!

QUEEN. Nevermore? Nevermore? But what am I to do? Are you saying because I'm mean I can no longer be beautiful? No, I won't believe it! I won't! I won't . . . (*begins to whimper*) . . . believe it . . .

MIRROR.
> Look but once at your disgrace
> For selfishness is on your face!

(*The QUEEN slowly turns and looks into the MIRROR, as we hear jangling chimes . . .*)

[MUSIC NO. 27: DOOM]

QUEEN. (*screams*) Ah! Look at my skin! It's wrinkled and shriveled! And my hair! My teeth! My eyes! My chin! No! No one must look at me! Not even you!

MIRROR.
> It is no use for you, my Queen
> For you're as ugly as you're mean!

QUEEN. I'll finish you for that!

(*The QUEEN slams her fists into the MIRROR and breaks it into a thousand pieces. We hear the shattering of glass. The QUEEN's chamber rolls off stage L., leaving the QUEEN onstage. The lights come up on the scene of grieving, with the DWARFS kneeling around SNOW WHITE's bier, their heads bowed in mourning. The QUEEN takes in the sight of the sad scene.*)

QUEEN. (*gasping*) I'll hide! That's what I'll do! (*as she runs off stage R.*) No one must look at me! I'll hide in darkness forever! (*She is gone. MUSIC.*)

(*The lights fade to a deep blue, and we hear THE PRINCE in the distance·*)

[MUSIC NO. 28: A PROMISE KEPT]

PRINCE. (*off-stage*)
REMEMBER WHEN
YOU DREAMED THE DAY
A PRINCE WOULD COME
FROM FAR AWAY?

AND YOU WERE TOLD
THE TIME WAS NEAR
AND VERY SOON
HE WOULD APPEAR

(*entering* L.)
HERE AM I
WEARING THE CAPE OF GOLD
AND BUCKLES OF SILVER
JUST AS YOU WERE TOLD

A PROMISE KEPT
FOR DREAMS PROVIDE
AWAKEN LOVE
AND BE MY BRIDE

(*The PRINCE comes to SNOW WHITE and kisses her, then crosses* D.L.)
AWAKEN LOVE
AND BE MY BRIDE!

(*Slowly, SNOW WHITE begins to stir. SCOTTY is the first to notice:*)

SCOTTY. Look! (*Chord.*)
SCRUBBER. She's moving! (*Chord.*)
FLUBBER. She's alive! (*Chord.*)
FRED. The kiss! (*Chord.*) It was the kiss! (*MUSIC.*)
BLUBBER. She's moving. (*Chord.*)
PEPITO. She's alive! (*Chord.*)
MOSQUITO. She's alive! (*Chord.*)

[MUSIC NO. 29: FINALE]

SNOW WHITE. (*waking*) I had such a sweet dream. I dreamed a prince kissed me My prince of the golden cape.

PRINCE It was no dream, Snow White. I am the Prince of Peridot. (*SNOW WHITE and the DWARFS kneel to his royalty, but he comes forward and raises SNOW WHITE from her curtsey, the DWARFS also rise*)

SNOW WHITE. But how did you find me?

PRINCE I heard a cry carried by the wailing of the wind, and it brought me here to you. Snow White, will you come with me and be my bride?

(*SNOW WHITE looks over to the DWARFS as they eagerly nod their approval. SNOW WHITE smiles and shyly nods· "yes."*)

SNOW WHITE. (*sings*)
I'M ALIVE AND I'M HAPPY AND FREE!
PRINCE.
I'M SO HAPPY INSIDE
THAT I'M SINGING FOR ME!
SNOW WHITE.
FOR MY TRUE LOVE HAS FOUND ME
MY FRIENDS ARE AROUND ME
SNOW WHITE AND PRINCE.
THE SUN IS ABOUT TO ARRIVE!
WE'RE ALIVE!
DWARFS.
THEY'RE ALIVE!
SNOW WHITE AND PRINCE
WE'RE ALIVE!
DWARFS
THEY'RE ALIVE!
ALL.
WE'RE ALIVE!

(*On the final chord, the PRINCE kisses SNOW WHITE romantically, as the curtain descends.*)

—THE HAPPY END—

[MUSIC NO 30: CURTAIN CALLS/FINALE ULTIMO]

During the BLACKOUT, the PRINCE exits L. SNOW WHITE exits into the tree-house. The doors are shut by two DWARFS.

Lights up, as the DWARFS are lined-up behind the log. Each, one-by-one, comes forward around the front of the log and bows quickly, FRED being the last

The DWARFS acknowledge the PRINCE, who enters and backs L.

The WOODSMAN enters D.R , comes to center and bows, retreating R., extending his arm to welcome the QUEEN from D.L.

The QUEEN comes to center, bows and retreats L., while extending her arm to acknowledge SNOW WHITE.

The DWARFS split C.; two DWARFS open the tree-house doors and SNOW WHITE steps forward. All acknowledge her, as two DWARFS assist her in standing on the log. She bows. The PRINCE comes to assist her off the log, lifting her by the waist to the floor; they walk down center, joined by QUEEN and WOODSMAN. Three DWARFS jump onto log; two DWARFS on either side US. of the Principals; all sing:

ALL.
AND NOW THAT YOU CAN YODEL
AND NOW THAT YOU CAN YODEL
YOU'LL DO MOST ANYTHING
YOU'LL YODEL THROUGH YOUR WINTER
AND YOU'LL YODEL INTO SPRING!

YO-DEL-AI-DI-O
YO-DEL-AI-DI-O
YO-DEL-AI-DI
YO-DEL-AI-DI . . .
YO-DEL-AI-DI-O-O-O-O-O

(On the final "O", the PRINCE picks up SNOW WHITE and carries her off R., as she waves goodbye to DWARFS and audience. DWARFS cluster together to wave goodbye to

departing PRINCE and SNOW WHITE, as the QUEEN angrily drags the frightened WOODSMAN off L.)

FINAL CURTAIN

(*NOTE: For the curtain calls in the Los Angeles production, the PRINCE entered last,* S.R., *on the final yodel, riding a live WHITE HORSE. He rode* DS. *of SNOW WHITE, rode* US. *of log, and assisted SNOW WHITE to mount behind him. On the singing of the last part of the final yodel, SNOW WHITE and the PRINCE rode off, waving to the DWARFS and the audience.*)

[MUSIC NO. 31: EXIT MUSIC]

PROP LIST

Stage Left;
Black bag, with two apples
Spectacles for first Old Lady
Beret for first Old Lady
Black scarf for second Old Lady
Oversized apple for "dream sequence"

Stage Right:
Two flower poles
Satin pillow
Small bouquet of flowers
Frying pan (two eggs in pan if possible)
7 lanterns
Ropes, axes, and shovels

Queen's Chamber:
Powder puff/box
Magic comb
Magic sash
Apple
Throne

In The House:
Small broom

Log:
One large wooden box, 6 ft. long, 2 ft. wide, 16 inches high. Top should be able to open to store lanterns, Snow White's broom, frying pan, etc. Box can be raked provided stage right end of box be higher than stage left. Rake should not exceed 2 inches Should lqok like a log lying in the forest.

COSTUME LIST

QUEEN·
Long black dress, encrusted on top with large, rich jewels to
    denote royalty
Long red cape with upstanding collar framing the back of the
    head
Black cloth helmet "coif," coming to the shoulders
Crown encrusted with gems

As 1st Old Woman:
Velcroed "choir" robe to cover dress (for fast-change)
Scarf — burlap shawl
Kerchief

As 2nd Old Woman.
Change of shawl
Hat to replace kerchief
Purse to carry apple

SNOW WHITE:
Young servant girl's dress of the period, with puffed sleeves
Fitted, laced bodice
Classic pumps

DWARFS:
Seven tunics }
Seven tights }   of different colors
Seven hats   }

Pepito:
Should suggest Spanish flair, vest with tassels, long stocking-
    cap, etc.

Scotty:
Tunic should be Scottish clan plaid, tam-o-shanter hat, matching
    plaid

PRINCE:
White fitted tunic
White tights

White boots
Gold lame cape
Princely crown

WOODSMAN:
Loose brown and/or green tunic with frayed, rough-cut edges
Wide brown leather belt
Brown or green tights
Brown leather boots
Brown and/or green stocking cap

On the facing page is a reproduction of the STUDY GUIDE
which has been used in "Childbills" (programs) for *Snow White
and the Seven Dwarfs.* It has proved very effective, and its use is
recommended.

SNOW WHITE STUDY GUIDE

The evil Queen, jealous of Snow White's beauty, has a Woodsman take her into the forest where he is to run a comb through her hair that will make her sleep forever.

The Woodsman, however, takes pity on the maid. Warning her never to return to the castle, he sets her free. Later, she is found by the Seven Dwarfs who, after fearing she might be there to steal their gold, learn of her plight and ask her to say with them.

Meanwhile, the Queen is told by her mirror that Snow White is still alive. Disguised as a vendor, she finds Snow White and gets her to try on a magic sash that renders the girl unconscious. She is chased away by the Dwarfs who discover and take off the sash They warn Snow White to be careful.

The Queen has many wiles, however. This time, armed with a magic apple she returns disguised as an old lady. Snow White, trustful by nature, bites of the apple and goes into a sleep. She is found by the desolate Dwarfs who, kneeling by her side, mourn her death.

While they express their sorrow, The Queen in her chambers has discovered the price of her wickedness. Due to her selfishness, her beauty is gone and cannot be regained. Maddened by this fact she runs off to "hide in darkness forever."

"Back in the forest, a prince in a golden cape appears. His kiss brings Snow White back to life and all ends happily.

1. The Queen is very angry. What is she angry about? Why is she so determined to get rid of Snow White?
2. Why is the mirror so important to the Queen?
3. What do you think about Snow White? Can you understand why the Woodsman didn't have the heart to kill her?
4. Snow White and the Seven Dwarfs are friends. Why is having a friend so important? What does friendship mean to you?
5. What happens to the Queen at the end of the play? Why does it happen? Why does she destroy the mirror?
6. What is the difference between Snow White and the Queen?
7. What do you think is the main idea of the play "Snow White?"

SET NOTES

The inside of the *TREE-HOUSE* represents an interior room painted in "storybook cottage" style, and warmly, brightly lit. It might represent the Dwarf's bedroom with seven little four-posters painted in perspective, or simply a living-room with a small sofa, windows, curtains, a lamp, etc. When the doors of the tree-house are shut, the outside represents the tree's bark and should not disclose the inner secret until the moment of its exposure to the audience.

The *LOG* is a long, rectangular box, approximately 6–7 feet long, painted in browns, greens, orange, etc., to represent tree-bark. It is hinged on the downstage side and holds many of the play's props, ie: after the Dwarf's entrance, in the clean-up scene, their lanterns are disposed of into the log-box. From it, Snow White takes the child-sized broom. The log prop also serves as the Dwarf's table, a bench for sitting and jumping-onto, and for Snow White's bier, etc.

The Queen's *CHAMBER PLATFORM*, which is on wheels, is painted to represent, or is actually covered in opulent looking draped fabric on a small flat On that wall is the shuttered *MIRROR*, which is opened only when the Queen addresses her alter-ego. There is also built onto the platform a seat for the Queen, throne-like and painted gold. Attached to the wall near the Mirror, is a small shelf to hold the Queen's powder, perfume atomizer, the comb, sash and apple, which are "created" onstage by the Queen and the Mirror. The Mirror, itself, is a tight swatch of see-through fabric (scrim) onto which a large, frightening face is suggested—but only suggested. The Mirror's voice is amplified over the sound-system. Lights behind the Mirror's "face" flicker as words come forth from it.

Although this was not done in past productions of SNOW WHITE, it is possible for the Queen's *CHAMBER PLATFORM* to be stationary, with the tree cut-out on that side of the stage placed in front of it. This cut-out might be on wheels to be taken into the wings when the Queen's scenes are in progress, and wheeled back to hide the Queen's PLATFORM when the forest alone is desired.

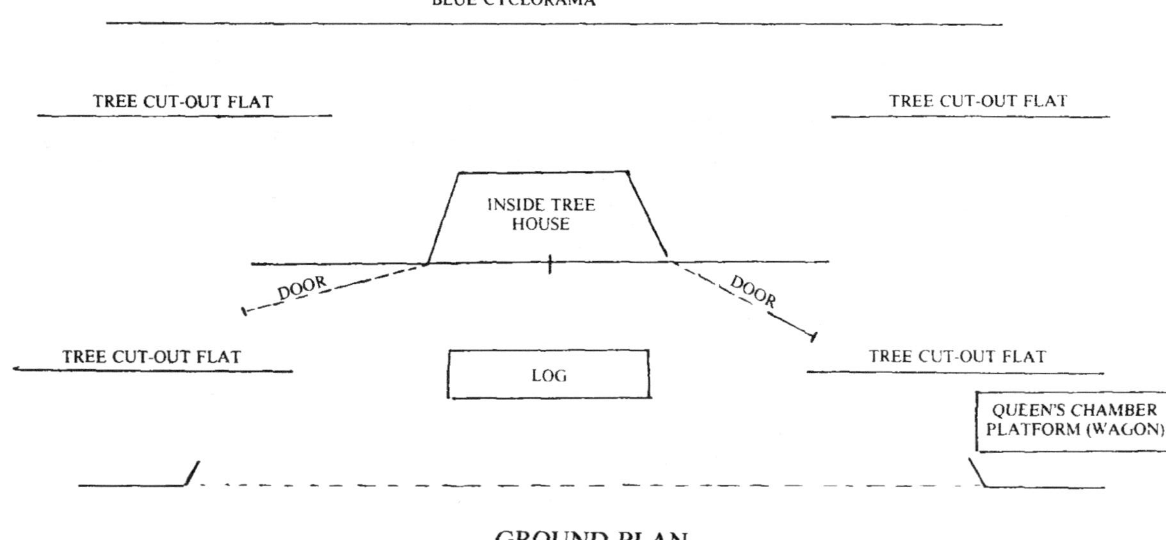

BLUE CYCLORAMA
TREE CUT-OUT FLAT
TREE CUT-OUT FLAT
INSIDE TREE HOUSE
DOOR
DOOR
TREE CUT-OUT FLAT
TREE CUT-OUT FLAT
LOG
QUEEN'S CHAMBER PLATFORM (WAGON)

GROUND PLAN

THE CRITICS SAID:

"Snow White and the Seven Dwarfs opened at Theater East two years ago and is still one of the best children's shows in town. Without slavishly following the Disney film (the dwarfs here are more like the Lost Boys in "Peter Pan" than little old men), Elsa Rael's script and Michael Valenti's score find much of the film's charm . . Snow White is fresh and unsticky . . . the Queen is superb—an elegant, damned creature whose desperate race to stay 'the fairest of them all' has contemporary relevance that won't escape sensitive kids . . ."

Dan Sullivan—*The New York Times*

". . . a fresh, delightful and inventive musical for, yes, wonder of wonders, children! I'm speaking of the Theater East's new vehicle, Snow White and the Seven Dwarfs, a thoroughly diverting and remarkably tuneful variation of the famed little classic . . . bursting with invention, originality and, perhaps most extraordinary of all, a musical score that ranks with much that is heard in the major Broadway houses. Composer Michael Valenti and his merry talented little band of colleagues are brightening many a wintry morning and afternoon with their musical."

Stanley Richards—*Players Magazine*

"In this lovely show, all those for whom the tale of Snow White, among other things, begins and ends in Walt Disney's interpretation will not be disappointed . . . a flawless production, Elsa Rael's book and lyrics are intelligent throughout . . . Michael Valenti's music is completely suitable . . ."

—*The Village Voice*

"Where most dramatizations of *Snow White* fail is in not convincing the children of the strong emotional bond between girl and dwarfs. If the audience believes Snow White loves the little people, and vice versa, it will love them, too, and relax, knowing she will be safe. Without this conviction, the children will be merely amused by the dwarfs and the point will be missed . . . Of all the *Snow White* productions I've seen, only two were fully satisfying in this basic respect: the Walt Disney animated film and a musical staged by the Gingerbread Players and written by Elsa Rael."

Muriel Broadman—
Understanding Your Child's Entertainment
(Harper and Row)

OTHER TITLES AVAILABLE FROM SAMUEL FRENCH

BEAUTY AND THE BEAST

Book by Peter Del Valle and John Ahearn
Music by Michael Valenti
Lyrics by Elsa Rael

Musical / 4m, 3f plus optional ensemble chorus / Simple Sets

This witty and sparkling version of the much loved classic has been seen in Town Hall and many other New York City venues as well as in summer, college and community theatres in Canada and the United states. The score brings together the creative team who wrote *Snow White and the Seven Dwarfs.*

"A show intended for children and yet there is not one iota of condescension or compromise in it. Michael Valenti's music can best be described as romantic light opera. Elsa Rael's lyrics possess a delicate simplicity and never talk down to the audience. Hardly typical children's fare."
– New York Theatre Review

"Has a magic all its own."
– The Chicago Tribune

"A beauty of a production."
– The Chicago Sun Times